Arto's
Big Move

To my family in the North & South.
With many thanks to all those who helped
along the way.

Arto's Big Move

Written and illustrated by

Monica Arnaldo

The North is a very
cold place to live.

Arto knew that firsthand:
He'd lived there his whole
life—and seven years was
a long time.

To keep warm up North, you have to wear lots and lots of layers. So every morning before leaving the house, Arto pulled on his thick wool socks,

stepped into his snug boots,

put on his knitted mittens,

wrapped himself in his big red coat,

and tugged on his favorite hat.

Under all those layers, Arto was cozy and comfortable and could spend hours out in the cold Northern weather, playing with his friends.

One day, while looking for his wool sock, Arto noticed something strange. A big stack of cardboard had appeared by the front door.

"M-o-o-o-m," he said, finding his mother in the front hall, "what's all this stuff?"

Arto's mother crouched down to face Arto. "Well, sweetie, they're boxes for the move."

She reminded him about her new job and how the family was going to live down South, just for a year. "You'll see. You'll love it there. In the South, it's always sunny and warm, and you won't need to wear your winter coat or hat."

Now Arto remembered. He looked at all his Northern things, hung with care along the wall. He made up his mind right then and there to hate the South.

When the day of the move finally came, Arto sat in his spot in the backseat and watched his parents fill the car with boxes. Finally, when they were ready to pull out of the driveway, they turned to check on Arto.

"Arto!" his father exclaimed. "You're going to cook like an egg wearing all those layers down South!"

Arto stared straight ahead. "I don't care."

His father glanced at his mother, then turned the key in the ignition. The little car rattled to a start, and the journey was underway.

As the minutes turned to hours, Arto felt his eyelids growing heavier. His soft, warm clothes made a cozy sort of nest between the boxes, and he eventually gave in to sleep.

They drove all night and all day, and then through the night again. On the morning of the third day, Arto woke with a stuffy, sweaty, overheated feeling. Heavy sunlight streamed in through his window. Curious, Arto peered outside.

The world beyond the window was completely different from anything Arto had ever seen. Instead of tall, spiky pine trees, the road was lined with short, prickly plants. Something was wrong with the houses, too. The roofs were flat, instead of pointed. Strange birds drifted past a sun that looked big and hot and mean.

Arto pulled his coat around his shoulders and didn't look out the window again for the rest of the ride.

For weeks after arriving at
the new house, Arto's parents
tried to help their son settle
in to the South, but nothing
seemed to work.

Every morning, before leaving
the house, Arto still pulled on
his thick wool socks and stepped
into his snug boots.

Then he put on his knitted mittens, wrapped himself in his big red coat, and tugged on his favorite hat.

Under all those layers, Arto couldn't spend too long in the sweltering Southern weather—but then, that didn't bother him too much, because he had no friends to play with anyway. With his hat pulled low over his eyes, Arto pretended he was still in the North.

The weeks drifted slowly and hotly by until, one day, something unexpected happened at school.

It was recess. As usual, Arto sat by himself in the shade of some prickly plants. He'd learned that these were called cacti. He still didn't like them, but at least they had needles instead of leaves, just like the pine trees in the North.

Suddenly, a shadow fell over Arto. He turned to see a pair of tanned feet in dusty Southern sandals.

The feet belonged to a girl he recognized from class.
She was even newer to the school than Arto. "Hello,"
said the girl. "I'm Ana." Arto made a face.

"...I like your hat," said Ana, a little more shyly. "You must
be from up North. I used to have one just like it, but I lost it
when we moved."

Arto was too surprised to be rude. "You lived up North?"
He looked at the girl more closely. She was wearing a breezy
white dress and had a cheery handkerchief tied around her
neck. Arto's hands felt clammy inside his mittens.

"Uh-huh. And the East and the West, too. My family moves
around a lot.

"So..." said Ana, "do you want to come play?"

Arto enjoyed the rest of recess quite a bit more than usual.

Over the next few months,
Arto spent less and less time
brooding by himself, and more
and more time playing with Ana
and their other new friends.

One day, while playing outside Ana's house, Arto noticed her looking at him strangely.

"What's wrong?" he asked, squinting his eyes to block out the sun.

Ana grabbed his hat. Then she told him to wait a minute and vanished inside.

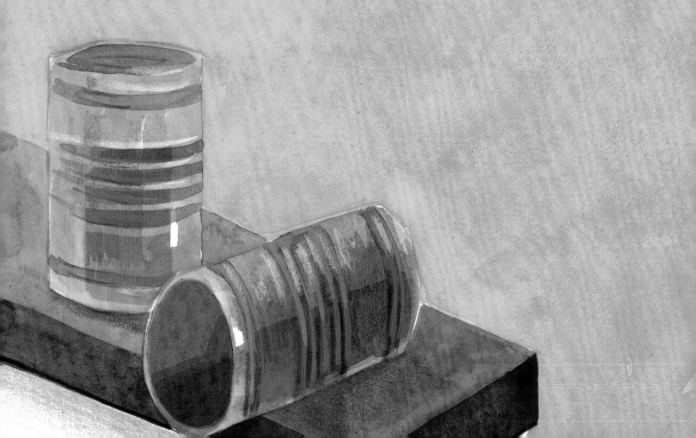

A cool shadow fell over Arto's face as Ana placed a wide-brimmed hat on his head.

"There! What do you think?"

"I can see without squinting!" Arto exclaimed.

Ana smiled and nodded. "Exactly! You can keep it, if you want."

Arto was too excited to thank Ana properly. "I can even make out my house in the distance!" he announced.

Arto couldn't wait to get home and show his parents his new hat.

"See you tomorrow!" he yelled as he ran back to his house.

But when Arto finally
reached his front door,
he could see something
was wrong.

The boxes were back.

Arto found his mother in the kitchen. "What's going on?"

"Oh, Arto, remember what we talked about? Our year here is nearly up! We'll be heading back up North soon, sweetie. Aren't you glad?"

At first Arto couldn't help but be excited—back to snow, back to ice! Back to skating and sledding and snow days! But then Arto's mother asked, "Arto, where did you get that hat?"

Arto slowly pulled Ana's hat off his head. He thought of his new friends. He thought of the prickly cacti and the beautiful songbirds that glided past the hot sun, and suddenly Arto wasn't sure how he felt about moving again.

Over the next few weeks, the little family said their good-byes, packed up their belongings once more, and piled into the creaking car to retrace their steps North. Arto thought hard about the year he had spent in the South. By the time they reached the familiar driveway of their old, snow-covered house, Arto knew what he wanted to do.

The North is a very
cold place to live.

Arto knew that firsthand:
He'd lived there most of his
life—and eight years was
a long time.

To keep warm up North, you have to wear lots and lots of layers. So every morning before leaving the house, Arto pulled on his thick wool socks,

stepped into his snug boots,

put on his knitted mittens,

wrapped himself in his big red coat,

and tugged on his favorite Southern hat.

Owlkids Books acknowledges the financial support of the Canada Council for the Arts, the Ontario Arts Council, the Government of Canada through the Canada Book Fund (CBF) and the Government of Ontario through the Ontario Media Development Corporation's Book Initiative for our publishing activities.

Published in Canada by   Published in the United States by
Owlkids Books Inc.   Owlkids Books Inc.
10 Lower Spadina Avenue   1700 Fourth Street
Toronto, ON M5V 2Z2   Berkeley, CA 94710

Library and Archives Canada Cataloguing in Publication

Arnaldo, Monica, author, illustrator
    Arto's big move / written and illustrated by Monica Arnaldo.

ISBN 978-1-77147-066-7 (bound)

    I. Title.

PS8601.R6543A78 2014   jC813'.6   C2014-900390-0

Library of Congress Control Number: 2014932637

Edited by: Karen Li and Jessica Burgess
Designed by: Barb Kelly and Alisa Baldwin

Manufactured in Shenzhen, China, in March 2014,
by C&C Joint Printing Co., (Guangdong) Ltd.
Job #HO0176

A   B   C   D   E   F

 Publisher of Chirp, chickaDEE and OWL
www.owlkidsbooks.com